CHRISTOPHER CHURCHMOUSE CLASSICS™

A LOAD OF TROUBLE

"Bread gained by deceit is sweet to a man;
but afterwards his mouth shall be filled with gravel"—Proverbs 20:17.

WRITTEN BY BARBARA DAVOLL
Pictures by Dennis Hockerman

A Sonflower Book

VICTOR BOOKS®

A DIVISION OF SCRIPTURE PRESS PUBLICATIONS INC.
USA CANADA ENGLAND

CHRISTOPHER CHURCHMOUSE CLASSICS

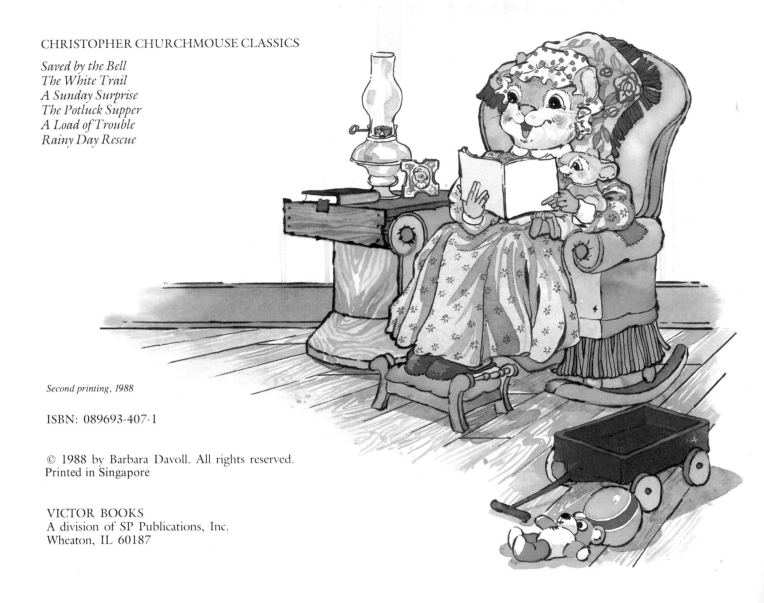

Second printing, 1988

ISBN: 089693-407-1

VICTOR BOOKS
A division of SP Publications, Inc.
Wheaton, IL 60187

A Word to Parents and Teachers

The Christopher Churchmouse Classics are a delightful series of character-building stories. As children read or hear these stories they will grow in their knowledge of God.

This book, *A Load of Trouble,* is about deceit. God says,
"Bread gained by deceit is sweet to a man;
but afterwards his mouth shall be filled with gravel"
—Proverbs 20:17.

All children will enjoy Christopher's antics as this little mouse finds that a a wagonload of crumbs turns into sawdust and becomes a load of trouble.

The Discussion Starters will help children think about the biblical truth and apply it to their own lives. Happy reading!

Christopher's Friend,

Barbara Davoll

Christopher Churchmouse did a double take as he was passing his cousin Sed's house. Standing right in front of the door was Sed's little green wagon. Now that wasn't too unusual because Sed used his wagon all the time to haul food and other things to his little hole in the wall. However, what really caught Chris' attention was what was in the wagon. It was full—right up to the brim—with delicious-looking bread crumbs!

Christopher looked both ways to see if anyone was watching, and then reached out and gathered a whole pawful of the crumbs. Stuffing them into his mouth he exclaimed to himself, "These are great!" (*Chomp, chomp.*) "Wonder where Sed got them?" (*Chomp, chomp.*)

Taking another mouthful he thought, *I'd like to have this load for myself.* He thought about how nice all the bread crumbs would be stored in his mother's pantry for the winter.

As Chris was thinking and chewing, Papa Churchmouse passed him on his way to work. Christopher swallowed quickly and brushed the crumbs from his face. Backing away from the wagon, he started whistling a little tune—looking *very* guilty.

Papa said, "Good morning, Chris. What are you doing today?"

"Oh, nothing, Papa," said Chris. "Just passing by on my morning walk."

"Hmmm," said Papa thoughtfully, looking at the wagon full of crumbs. "You weren't thinking of eating some of Sed's crumbs, were you?"

6

How can he always know what I'm thinking? thought Christopher. But aloud he said, "Oh, no, Papa." *At least I'm not thinking of eating them now,* he continued softly to himself. But deep inside his heart he knew that wasn't true. He was thinking of getting the crumbs for himself, and, as usual, his wise papa knew it.

"Well, be sure you aren't deceiving yourself," said Papa.

"What does that mean?" asked Christopher.

"Deceive means 'to fool somebody' or 'to cause somebody to believe an untruth,' " said Papa. "In a way, it's just like lying."

"Why, Papa," exclaimed Christopher, "you know I wouldn't lie!"

"I hope not, but you might deceive or fool yourself. Remember, Pastor Shepherd told the people a few weeks ago, 'The heart is deceitful and desperately wicked.' "

"Yes, Papa, I remember," said Christopher. "I'll be careful not to deceive."

"See that you don't, Chris. Have a good day," said Papa, giving him a pat on his head and hurrying off with his lunch bucket.

After Papa left, Christopher looked hungrily at the wagonload of crumbs.

Suppose, he thought, *that I replace Sed's crumbs, say, with—sawdust. Yeah, that's a good idea. After all, that wouldn't be stealing, for I would be giving him something he needs. He probably has enough crumbs, and I don't have any. I have plenty of sawdust from when we made our pantry bigger. A mouse can always use sawdust. That's what I'll do. He'll never care. In fact, he'll be glad to have sawdust when he doesn't have any of his own.*

And with that Christopher started to pull the wagon full of crumbs toward his own house. As he did, he remembered for a minute what Papa had said about deceit. Papa had said deceit was causing someone to believe an untruth, and that was what he was doing. But Chris quickly put that thought out of his mind. He just concentrated on getting the wagon home without being seen.

Working quickly when he got there, he stored the bread crumbs in some little boxes Mama had in the pantry. Then he filled the wagon with

the sawdust and returned it to Sed's house. He left the wagon just where he had found it. No one saw him.

Great! thought Chris, dusting himself off. *No one saw me. I'm sure Sed will never notice, and if he does, he'll think he made the mistake himself.*

Very pleased, Christopher went home to have his tea. He was very proud to think how smart he'd been.

Just as Mama was pouring the tea there was a knock at the door.

"Who can that be?" wondered Mama. "Chris, answer the door. I have to get back to the kitchen."

Opening the door, Christopher saw, to his surprise, his cousin Sed with the wagon full of sawdust. Chris' heart started to beat faster. *What on earth? Does he know? How did he find out?* Christopher thought in astonishment.

"C-come in, Sed," he stammered aloud.

"Thank you, Christopher," replied Sed. "I've brought you a present."

"You-you have?" stuttered Christopher.

"Yes. I've brought you a whole wagonload of bread crumbs. I hauled them up from the kitchen last night. I got another load today and thought I'd share it with you."

"Oh, how nice, but—are you sure—you want to?" floundered Christopher, feeling worse every minute.

"Sure, you're my favorite cousin, aren't you? What's a family for, if not to help one another?" Sed squeaked happily.

"Wh—wh—that's kind of you, Sed. I'll unload them right in the pantry and . . ."

"Oh, I see you're just having tea. That's great! Then I can watch you enjoy them," Sed explained. With that Sed put a big scoop of the sawdust on Christopher's plate.

"Yes, great," said Christopher miserably, and he sat down before the plate of sawdust. "Would you like some?" he asked weakly.

"Oh, no, thank you. I ate plenty while I was loading the wagon. They're delicious!"

Putting some in his mouth, Chris began to choke it down.

"How do you like them?" asked Sed.

"Delicious!" choked Christopher, as he took a gulp of tea to wash the sawdust down.

13

Christopher had never felt more miserable in his life. Papa had been so right. "The heart is deceitful," and Christopher had deceived not only Sed but also himself in thinking such

a trick was all right. How terrible Chris felt to know he had deceived Sed in such a mean way. And Sed had been so kind to him too.

"Choke—gasp—choke," sputtered Christopher.

"Why, Chris, what's the matter?" asked Sed, jumping up to pound his choking cousin on the back. "Don't you like the bread crumbs?"

By now tears were streaming down the face of the guilty little mouse. "No! No, I don't!" he squeaked unhappily.

"You don't?" Sed questioned in wonder. "Why, I thought you'd like them. I thought . . ."

"Stop!" said Christopher, putting up his hand to still Sed's questions. "Oh, I have been so naughty but I'm very, very sorry, Sed," cried Christopher, fishing out his handkerchief from his back pocket and blowing his nose loudly.

"Why, Chris, whatever is wrong?" asked Sed. He came over to Chris and patted him on the shoulder.

"Deceit is wrong!" said Christopher.

"What's deceit?" asked Sed curiously.

"Deceit is causing someone to believe an untruth," said the unhappy little mouse, wiping his eyes. "It's the same thing as lying."

"I see," Sed replied. "But what does that have to do with my bread crumbs?"

"They aren't bread crumbs," squeaked Christopher.

"What do you mean, not bread crumbs! They are too! They're nice bread crumbs from the kitchen. I had some myself and I know."

"No, they're not," interrupted Christopher. "I mean, they were, but they're not now."

"What *are* you talking about, Christopher?" exclaimed Sed, beginning to get angry. "These most cer-

tainly are bread crumbs," he said emphatically, stepping over to the table and taking a pawful. "They most certainly are! Why, they're very good bread crumbs," he insisted, stuffing his pawful into his mouth.

The moment Sed put the sawdust in his mouth he began to choke and cough. Christopher rushed to hand him a cup of cooled tea to drink.

"Here!" Chris said, handing it to him. "I tried to tell you they're not crumbs. They're sawdust."

"Sawdust!" shrieked Sed, taking a big gulp and coughing.

17

"Yes, sawdust," said Christopher weakly. "I was trying to tell you that I exchanged your bread crumbs for some sawdust. I deceived you, Sed. I wanted you to think they were still bread crumbs. I took your crumbs and stored them in our pantry and I replaced the crumbs with some sawdust. It almost worked too. I almost deceived you, and it was very wrong."

"What's wrong?" asked Mama, coming into the room suddenly.

"Oh, no," mumbled Christopher.
"Now I'm really in for it. Deceit is
wrong," he said for the second time.
Then he explained to Mama how he
had fooled Sed by exchanging the
crumbs for sawdust. He also explained
what Papa had said about deceit.

When Christopher had finished talking, Mama came over and put her arm around his shoulders.

"Well, Son, I certainly think you have learned a lesson today."

Christopher nodded his head. He was glad his mama was so understanding, but he knew he must still ask Sed's forgiveness.

"You see, Sed, I deceived you because I caused you to believe an untruth. Will you forgive me?" asked Christopher.

21

"Of course I will," squeaked Sed, giving him a hug. Christopher was so happy to be forgiven that he felt another tear slip down his cheek. Wiping his eyes, he looked at his mama.

"And I forgive you too," said Mama, taking him in her arms and giving him a big hug.

Christopher had learned a very important lesson that day. God says in His Word, "Bread gained by deceit is sweet to a man, but afterward his mouth will be filled with gravel" (Proverbs 20:17).

Well, in this case, sawdust, Christopher thought to himself.

22

DISCUSSION STARTERS

1. What did Christopher find in front of his cousin's door?
2. What did Papa Churchmouse say "deceive" means?
3. How is deceiving someone just like lying?
4. What did Christopher do with the load of bread crumbs?
5. Do you think Sed was a good cousin to Christopher?
   Why do you think he was?
6. Did Christopher make things right with Sed?
   How?